Yorkshire Terriers

Stephanie Finne

**Checkerboard
Library**

An Imprint of Abdo Publishing
www.abdopublishing.com

www.abdopublishing.com

Published by Abdo Publishing, a division of ABDO, PO Box 398166, Minneapolis, MN 55439.
Copyright © 2015 by Abdo Consulting Group, Inc. International copyrights reserved in all
countries. No part of this book may be reproduced in any form without written permission from
the publisher. Checkerboard Library™ is a trademark and logo of Abdo Publishing.

Printed in the United States of America, North Mankato, Minnesota.
102014
012015

Cover Photo: iStockphoto
Interior Photos: Alamy p. 11; Corbis p. 10; iStockphoto pp. 1, 5, 6–7, 12–13, 16–17, 19, 21;
    SuperStock pp. 9, 15

Series Coordinator: Tamara L. Britton
Editors: Megan M. Gunderson, Bridget O'Brien
Production: Jillian O'Brien

Library of Congress Cataloging-in-Publication Data

Finne, Stephanie, author.
  Yorkshire terriers / Stephanie Finne.
      pages cm. -- (Dogs)
  Audience: Ages 8-12.
  Includes index.
    ISBN 978-1-62403-677-4
  1. Yorkshire terrier--Juvenile literature. 2. Toy dogs--Juvenile literature. I. Title.
  SF429.Y6F56 2015
    636.76--dc23
                         2014025388

Contents

The Dog Family

The **American Kennel Club (AKC)** recognizes 180 **breeds** of dogs. All of these dogs are members of the family **Canidae**. The name comes from the Latin word for "dog," which is *canis*.

Dogs and people have lived and worked together for more than 12,000 years. Their relationship began when early humans trained wolf pups to help them hunt. Modern dogs descended from these early pups.

Eventually, humans developed different breeds to assist with other tasks. Working breeds pulled carts and sleds. Herding breeds drove animals. Yorkshire terriers were bred to hunt **rodents**. Today, they are companion dogs.

The Yorkshire terrier

Yorkshire Terriers

In the 1800s, a group of weavers moved from Scotland to Yorkshire, England. They brought along terriers to keep textile mills free of **rodents**. These dogs included clydesdale and paisley terriers.

These terriers were **bred** with black-and-tan English terriers to create the waterside terrier. This dog first appeared in a dog show in 1861. At that time, the breed was known as the broken-haired Scottish terrier. In 1870, the breed became known as the Yorkshire terrier, or Yorkie.

Around this time, Yorkshire terriers were brought to the United States. The breed was recognized by the **AKC** in 1885. It was one of the first 25 breeds recognized by the club. In 1954, the Yorkshire Terrier Club of America was formed.

Today, the Yorkshire terrier is the sixth most popular breed in the United States.

What They're Like

Yorkshire terriers are small dogs with big personalities! They can be wonderful lap dogs. But they have terrier traits that make them independent, stubborn, and fierce. They are confident and alert, and they have a strong will.

Energetic Yorkies need daily exercise and room to run. If they don't get enough exercise, they can get into trouble! A bored Yorkie will come up with its own entertainment. This can include digging and barking. It can also mean shaking and shredding things.

The Yorkshire terrier will bond with its caregiver. However, these dogs may not be suited for families with small children. Young children and Yorkies can easily hurt each other.

Yorkies need exercise to burn off their excess energy.

Yorkies can be very demanding! They want all of your attention all of the time. They don't want to be alone. Yorkies are challenging, but their charms make them entertaining pets.

Coat and Color

Yorkshire terriers have a beautiful single coat. They do not have an **undercoat**. This means the **breed** is not protected from weather. Yorkies should not be exposed to extreme conditions.

The color, texture, and quality of the Yorkie's coat is important. The glossy, silky coat should be thick, straight, and fine. The Yorkie's hair is long. The hair on the Yorkie's head is often tied up in one or two topknots to keep it out of the dog's eyes.

The puppy cut

The Yorkie's coat is blue and tan. On the body, the coat should be a dark steel blue. There should be no fawn, bronze, or black hair. The Yorkie's head and legs are tan. The tan hair should be darker at the roots and lighter toward the tips.

Many Yorkie owners trim the hair to floor length so their dogs can more easily move. It also gives them a neater appearance. Yorkies that are not show dogs often have a short haircut called the "puppy cut." The shorter hair is easier to groom and keep clean.

The full show coat

Size

Yorkshire terriers are toy-sized dogs. They are just eight to nine inches (20 to 23 cm) tall. They weigh about seven pounds (3 kg).

The Yorkie's small head is flat on top. It is topped with small, pointed ears. The ears are always erect. Medium-sized, dark eyes sit aside a medium-length **muzzle**. It is tipped with a black nose.

The Yorkie's compact body rests on straight legs. The front and rear legs are the same length, so the dog's short back is level. The legs end in round paws that have black toenails.

The Yorkshire terrier has a **docked** tail. It is carried slightly higher than the back. Due to their small size, Yorkshire terriers are fragile. They may act terrier tough, but their tiny bodies should be handled with care!

Is your Yorkie making a honking sound? This is called pharyngeal (fah-ruhn-GEE-uhl) gag reflex, or reverse sneezing. This harmless condition often occurs when the dog is excited.

Care

Like all dogs, Yorkshire terriers need to see a veterinarian once a year. The vet will check the dog's health and give it necessary **vaccines**. Dogs that will not have puppies can be **spayed** or **neutered**.

Yorkies can live in the city or the country. As long as they get exercise and love, they will be happy. Daily walks will be good for your Yorkie. These dogs love to run and play.

Grooming is a big part of caring for a Yorkie. Yorkies do not **shed** in seasons. Their hair tends to break instead. So, the coat must be brushed every day. This will help to avoid tangles and **mats**. Gently untangle any knots before brushing the hair.

Many owners occasionally bathe their Yorkies. Be sure to use a shampoo made especially for dogs to help keep the coat healthy. Those black toenails will also need trimming.

Do not forget to brush your Yorkie's teeth. Yorkies are prone to tooth decay and gum disease. Brushing the teeth every day will help keep your Yorkie healthy.

When bathing your Yorkie, avoid getting shampoo in its ears and eyes.

Feeding

It is important for Yorkies to get a balanced diet. The best food is labeled "complete and balanced." These foods have all of the **protein** and **nutrients** your dog needs.

Yorkies have smaller mouths and stomachs than large **breeds**. They need food that is small enough to chew easily. But the food should still contain all the nutrients the dog needs. This can make finding a dog food difficult.

There are foods specially made for small dogs. The most popular foods are dry foods. They are made so each piece is packed with nutrients. There are also semimoist foods and canned foods. These have more moisture for dogs that need softer food.

As puppies, these small dogs will need to be fed four to six times a day. Adult Yorkshire terriers should be fed twice a day. Be sure to ask your vet about the type and amount of food to feed your Yorkie. He or she can also suggest treats. Along with food, provide fresh water for your dog every day!

Research your Yorkie's food to determine its calorie content. Then you can decide the proper portion to maintain a healthy weight.

Things They Need

In addition to care and grooming, your Yorkshire terrier will have other needs. Yorkies enjoy a crate to sleep in. Your dog should be able to stand up and turn around in its crate. Yorkies like a crate that feels like a cozy den.

Your new pet needs a collar with an identification tag. The tag should have your contact information in case your Yorkie gets lost. Your vet can also insert a **microchip** in your dog.

Don't forget that Yorkies need a lot of exercise! You will need a leash to walk your Yorkie. But, the Yorkie's fragile throat can be injured when the leash pulls on the collar. So, a harness may be a better option. A harness goes around the Yorkie's body, taking pressure off of the neck and throat.

Yorkies love toys! These dogs enjoy playing with balls, ropes, and chew toys. Yorkies are intelligent dogs, and toys keep them entertained.

These things are all important. But most of all, a Yorkie needs a loving family, **socialization**, and training. This will result in a happy, well-behaved dog.

A coat will help keep a Yorkie warm in winter.

Puppies

Full-grown Yorkies are so small they seem to be permanent puppies! But by six months of age, they are adult dogs. They can then have puppies of their own.

After mating, a female Yorkie is **pregnant** for about 63 days. There will be two to four puppies in her **litter**. They drink their mother's milk to grow.

The newborn puppies are blind and deaf. They can see and hear after two weeks. At three weeks of age, the puppies begin taking their first steps. When they are 8 to 12 weeks old, the Yorkie puppies are ready for a loving home.

Is the Yorkshire terrier the right dog for your family? If so, find a trusted **breeder**. A good breeder will test parent dogs for health problems before breeding them. So, you will know the Yorkie puppy is healthy.

Yorkshire terrier puppies are born with dark hair. They develop their tan coloring as they get older.

When you get your puppy home, begin basic obedience training. **Socialize** your puppy by introducing it to different people and places. A well cared for Yorkshire terrier will be a loving family companion for about 15 years.

Glossary

American Kennel Club (AKC) - an organization that studies and promotes interest in purebred dogs.

breed - a group of animals sharing the same ancestors and appearance. A breeder is a person who raises animals. Raising animals is often called breeding them.

Canidae (KAN-uh-dee) - the scientific Latin name for the dog family. Members of this family are called canids. They include wolves, jackals, foxes, coyotes, and domestic dogs.

dock - to cut short, especially a tail or ears.

litter - all of the puppies born at one time to a mother dog.

mat - a tangled mass.

microchip - an electronic circuit placed under an animal's skin. A microchip contains identifying information that can be read by a scanner.

muzzle - an animal's nose and jaws.

neuter (NOO-tuhr) - to remove a male animal's reproductive glands.

nutrient - a substance found in food and used in the body. It promotes growth, maintenance, and repair.

pregnant - having one or more babies growing within the body.

protein - a substance which provides energy to the body and serves as a major class of foods for animals. Foods high in protein include cheese, eggs, fish, meat, and milk.

rodent - any of several related animals that have large front teeth for gnawing. Common rodents include mice, squirrels, and beavers.

shed - to cast off hair, feathers, skin, or other coverings or parts by a natural process.

socialize - to adapt an animal to behaving properly around people or other animals in various settings.

spay - to remove a female animal's reproductive organs.

undercoat - short hair or fur partly covered by longer protective fur.

vaccine (vak-SEEN) - a shot given to prevent illness or disease.

Websites

To learn more about Dogs, visit **booklinks.abdopublishing.com**. These links are routinely monitored and updated to provide the most current information available.

Index